MORE SPECIAL OFFERS FOR MR MEN AND LITTLE MISS READERS

In every Mr Men and Little Miss book like this one,
sticker and activity books, you will find a special token.
will send you a gift of your cho
Choose either a Mr Men or Little Miss poster, **or** a
double sided full colour bedroom doc

Return this page **with six tokens per gift required** to:
Marketing Dept., MM / LM, World International Ltd.,
PO Box 7, Manchester, M19 2HD

Your name:________________________ Age: ______

Address: ________________________________

____

____________________Postcode: ____________

Parent / Guardian Name (Please Print)____________________

100 mm
250 mm
ENTRANCE FEE
3 SAUSAGES
MR. GREEDY

Please tape a 20p coin to your request to cover part post and package cost

I enclose six tokens per gift, and 20p please send me:-

Posters:-	Mr Men Poster	☐	Little Miss Poster	☐
Door Hangers -	Mr Nosey / Muddle	☐	Mr Greedy / Lazy	☐
	Mr Tickle / Grumpy	☐	Mr Slow / Busy	☐
	Mr Messy / Quiet	☐	Mr Perfect / Forgetful	☐
	L Miss Fun / Late	☐	L Miss Helpful / Tidy	☐
	L Miss Busy / Brainy	☐	L Miss Star / Fun	☐

Please Tick Appropriate Box

20p

Stick 20p here please

Collect six of these tokens
You will find one inside every
Mr Men and Little Miss book
which has this special offer.

1 TOKEN

We may occasionally wish to advise you of other Mr Men gifts.
If you would rather we didn't please tick this box ☐

Offer open to residents of UK, Channel Isles and Ireland only

MR. WORRY

by Roger Hargreaves

WORLD INTERNATIONAL

Poor Mr Worry.

Whatever happened, he worried about it.

If it rained, he worried that his roof was going to leak.

If it didn't rain, he worried that all the plants in his garden were going to die.

If he set off shopping, he worried that the shops would be shut when he got there.

And when the shops weren't shut when he got there, he worried that he was spending too much money shopping.

And when he got home with his shopping, he worried that he'd left something behind, or that something had fallen out of his basket on the way home.

And when he got home, and discovered that he hadn't left anything behind, and that nothing had fallen out of his basket on the way home, he worried that he'd bought too much.

And then he worried about where to put it all.

Life was just one long worry for poor Mr Worry.

One day, he went for a walk.

He was worried that he might walk too far and not be able to get home, but on the other hand, he was worried that if he didn't walk far enough, he wouldn't get enough exercise.

He hurried along worrying.

Or you could say, he worried along hurrying.

He met Mr Bump.

"I'm very worried about you," he said.

"Why's that?" asked Mr Bump.

"I'm worried that one of these days you might hurt yourself," he said.

"Don't you worry your head about that," replied Mr Bump.

And went off.

Tripping over his own feet.

Mr Worry went on.

He met Mr Noisy.

"I'm very worried about you," he said.

"Why's that?" asked Mr Noisy.

"I'm worried that you might lose your voice," said Mr Worry.

"Don't you worry your head about that," said Mr Noisy.

And went off.

CLUMP! CLUMP! CLUMP!

Mr Worry went on.

He met Mr Greedy.

"I'm very worried about you," he said.

"Why's that?" asked Mr Greedy.

"I'm worried that you might eat too much and be sick," explained Mr Worry.

"Me?" replied Mr Greedy.

"Eat too much?"

"Impossible!"

And went off.

For lunch.

Mr Worry went on.

He met a wizard.

"Hello," said the wizard. "Who are you?"

"I'm Mr Worry."

"And you look it," commented the wizard.

"Tell you what," he went on, for he was a helpful sort of a wizard. "Why don't you go home and write down every single thing that you're worried about, and I'll make sure that none of these things ever happen."

He smiled.

"And then you won't have anything to worry about will you?"

Mr Worry smiled.

It was the first time he'd smiled in a long time.

In fact, it was the first time he'd smiled that year.

He hurried home in great excitement.

When he got home, he sat down to write out all the things that worried him.

Every single thing.

It was a long list!

And then he went to bed and had the best night's sleep he'd had in years.

The following morning, the wizard came round to collect Mr Worry's list.

"My goodness me," he said when he saw the size of it.

"However," he said, "leave it to me. I'll go off and make sure that none of these things ever happen."

And off he went.

"Nothing to worry about now," he called over his shoulder. "Nothing at all!"

Mr Worry heaved a sigh of relief.

That day was the first day in Mr Worry's life that he didn't have a single thing to worry about.

And the next day.

And the day after.

And the day after that.

On Monday, Tuesday, Wednesday, Thursday, Friday, Saturday and Sunday, Mr Worry didn't have a care in the world.

But . . .

On Monday morning he was a worried man.

Oh dear.

What do you think was worrying him?

Can you guess?

He went to see the wizard.

"Oh dear," said the wizard when he saw him standing on his doorstep. "What's worrying you?"

"I'll tell you," said Mr Worry.

"I'm worried because I don't have anything to worry about!"

And he went home.

To worry about not having anything to worry about!